# YES, YOU CAN

Written by **Kathryn Royle** · Illustrated by **Sarah Schaller**

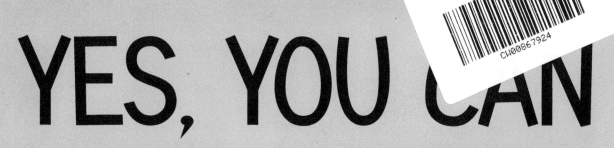

Archway Publishing books may be ordered through booksellers or by contacting:

Archway Publishing
1663 Liberty Drive
Bloomington, IN 47403
www.archwaypublishing.com
1 (888) 242-5904

Because of the dynamic nature of the Internet, any web addresses or links contained in this book may have changed since publication and may no longer be valid. The views expressed in this work are solely those of the author and do not necessarily reflect the views of the publisher, and the publisher hereby disclaims any responsibility for them.

Any people depicted in stock imagery provided by Getty Images are models, and such images are being used for illustrative purposes only.
Certain stock imagery © Getty Images.

ISBN: 978-1-4808-7583-8 (sc)
ISBN: 978-1-4808-7584-5 (hc)
ISBN: 978-1-4808-7582-1 (e)

Print information available on the last page.

Archway Publishing rev. date: 11/11/2019

This book is dedicated to my beautiful and spirited daughters, Chanda and Joclyn. I'm so proud of them for loving themselves and others after the sudden loss of their father. They were my baby birds with broken wings and through faith and support from family and friends, they found the strength to "sing".

I also dedicate this book to those who have been broken, crushed, or just a little damaged. May they all realize what talents and gifts they have to offer themselves and others while they journey out of their hurt and pain and always remember to pay it forward.

Very, very, early one morning...

Beaver woke up with a terrible toothache! He couldn't gather sticks with that *nawing* pain.

Brother beaver quickly swam up to him and said excitedly, "I could carry sticks if you show me where to go!"

Beaver did not want any help. He wanted to do it all by himself. But he was soooo eager to build his damn that he agreed to work with Brother Beaver.

So they did.

Beaver got so busy directing his brother on where to get sticks that he forgot all about his tooth ache!

They built their damn

FASTER and BIGGER

than he ever imagined.

Beaver was very happy. He gave his brother a big "high five" and said, "Thank you, brother!"

Just then; out of the corner of his eye,

Beaver saw something **very big**...

Bear was wandering by the side of the creek.

"We built a damn this morning!" Beaver proudly announced.
"What are YOU going to do today Bear?

"I'm trying to find some fish and honey," Bear mumbled.

Beaver eagerly said,

"I can help you!"

"I just gathered sticks and I know
right where the fish are!"

Without giving it a second thought, Beaver took
off to get them."

Just then, a big swarm of bees went

buzzing by;

so Bear followed them to the honey.

When he came back to the side of the creek
there was a big fish just waiting for him.
"Awwhhhhh...Thanks Beaver!"

As Bear was sitting
on a rock enjoying
his fish....

Snake slithered by and scared Bear right off his rock!

Bear was very nervous about being around snake.

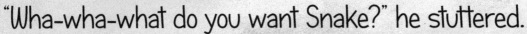

"Wha-wha-what do you want Snake?" he stuttered.

"I'm **sssssimply** trying to shed my old **sssssskin,**" he hissed.

Bear stated very decisively; "I don't like snakes. But I think I can help."

"You *sssssink sssssoooo?*" snake asked.

"Yep," Bear said confidently," I'm BIG and STRONG and I can get that old skin off in *one tug!*"

And he did.

"Ahhhhhh," snake sighed in relief. "That feelsssss good! Thanksssss Bear." And with that he slithered away.

Hiding nearby in the bushes...

Fox snuck up on Snake and grabbed him by the neck. He squeezed tighter and tighter with every word and yelled,
"STOP TRYING TO COPY ME!"

"You are **slithery** and I am **sly**. Those words both start with s!" Fox yelled.

"I am NOT a copycat, you sssssssilly Fox! We are nothing alike!" Hissed snake. "Look at *yoursssself* and then look at me!"

Fox suddenly noticed his reflection in the calm water of the creek.

He stopped being angry and started to admire himself. "You're right snake! I look good. You're just an ugly snake who's **not worth getting mad about.**" And with that he tossed Snake to the side and set him free.

As fox was strutting away feeling good about himself, he accidently stepped on...

Baby Bird who was struggling to pull a worm from the ground.

"Ouch! You mean nasty Fox! You broke my wing!" whined Baby Bird, "Now I'll never be able to fly back up to my nest!"

Mama bird was nowhere to be found.

Baby Bird was all by herself.

She continued to cry and pout...feeling sorry for herself.

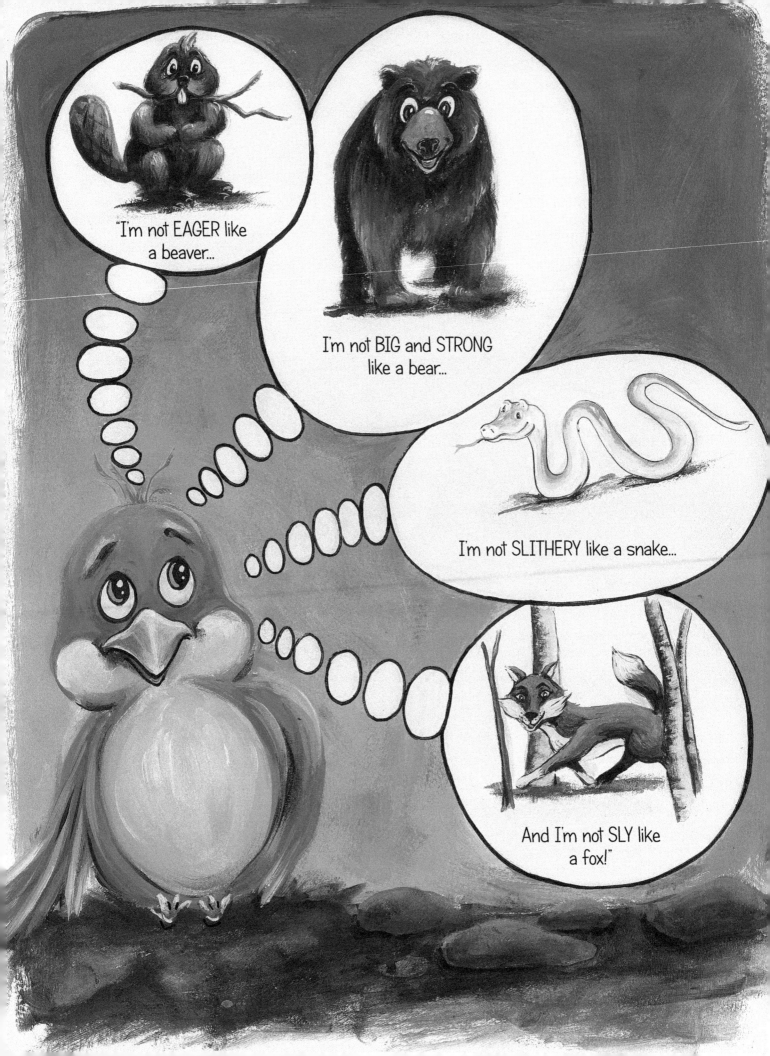

Fox crouched down and stared Baby Bird

straight
in
the
eyes,

and without feeling a bit sorry for her he said, "Yeah, yeah...so what? So I broke your wing; what's the big deal? You can still sing."

Baby Bird thought about it for a minute and stopped feeling sorry for herself. And then;

very, very, late that evening...

Baby Bird tweeted the
most beautiful sounds.
Beaver, Bear, Snake, and Fox
all came to see where the
tweets were coming from.
When they saw Baby Bird
on the ground, they
wanted to help her.

"Can we lift you up into your nest so we can hear you better?" They asked.

Baby Bird replied with a comforting sigh.

"Yes, you can."

## About the Author

KATHRYN ROYLE is a writer and a mother of two. Her book entertains and engages both the reader and the child. She uses simple examples to teach some life lessons. Kathryn currently resides in Green Bay, Wisconsin.

## About the Illustrator

SARAH SCHALLER is a career artist and mother of two. She is inspired by nature and her vivid artwork brings depth to each page. Her use of self-expression brings the characters alive. Sarah lives in Green Bay, Wisconsin.

Lightning Source UK Ltd.
Milton Keynes UK
UKHW051249281119
354389UK00005B/76/P